Family, Friends, and Flowers

By

Linda L. Bryant

Illustrations:

Chanel Davis

AuthorHouse™
1663 Liberty Drive
Bloomington, IN 47403
www.authorhouse.com
Phone: 833-262-8899

This book is printed on acid-free paper.

Interior Image Credit: Chanel Davis

ISBN: 979-8-8230-2797-7 (sc)
979-8-8230-2798-4 (e)

Library of Congress Control Number: 2024911429

Print information available on the last page.

Published by AuthorHouse 06/05/2024

authorHOUSE®

Family, Friends, and Flowers

My name is Brielle, and I like spending time
with my family, friends, and flowers.
Mostly during the daytime hours.

We meet in my Auntie Girl's backyard.

It looks like a beautiful picture or a greeting card.

3

Uncle Andre is a farmer who plants flowers at Auntie Girl's place.
Here, he stands proudly with a smile on his face.

4

We cook lots of food and some food we grill.
We play and enjoy each other, expressing how we feel.

We have so much food, and we pile it on our plates.
Auntie Girl comes to the table with our favorite lemon cake!

7

Off goes our shoes, and the grass tickles our feet.
We also see the sunshine and enjoy its beaming heat.

8

We play in the sprinkler, and the water goes very high!
We have so much fun as the water nearly touches the sky.

9

There are red birds, blue birds, and butterflies.
Some are on the fence, and some are in the sky.
We see rabbits hiding while standing still in their places.
We laugh so hard until smiles are stuck on our faces.

There is only one more thing I must say.
When I am with family, friends, and flowers,
I always have a really <u>great day</u>!

The End

Author's Bio

With a career transition from a Registered Respiratory Therapist to a creative writer, Linda L. Bryant's dedication to her craft is evident. Her music, available on Spotify and YouTube under her name and the title, "Never Hold Back on My Praise," Is a testament to her spiritual beliefs, life experiences, and passion. Linda's work resonates with young and older readers and listeners, making it accessible to many audiences. Her early readers' children's books are a powerful tool for promoting good behavior for children and encouraging positive change in their lives.

psalmwriter4g@gmail.com

https://psalmwriter4g.weebly.com

Acknowledgments:

The author sincerely appreciates
Chanel Davis, illustrator
Chanel@mcguffey@yahoo.com, and
the main character, Brielle.

Printed in the United States
by Baker & Taylor Publisher Services